Moving Out

Written by Sally Prue
Illustrated by Martin Remphry

1. THE HOUSE IN THE HOLE

Dan Dare, Pilot of the Future, stood proudly before his enemy, the green-headed Mekon. To speak the truth was certain death – but Dan Dare could not tell a lie.

"Put that comic away now, Philip," said Mum, "we're just coming into our station."

Philip reluctantly rolled up his *Eagle* comic and pushed it into the deep pocket of his raincoat. Through the smoke that blew past the train window, the countryside looked grey and even soggier than London.

The spring of 1951 had been the wettest anyone could remember and the rain was still lashing down.

The *diddle-dee-DEE* of the train wheels faded into a great *shhhhh!* of brakes, and Philip clambered down the steps from the carriage and hurried after Mum and Dad.

Mum looked left and right.

"This was the right station, wasn't it?" she asked.

Across the road was a soggy field and a river, and not much else.

"Where's our new house, Dad?" asked Philip.

They had to catch a bus to get there. Philip wiped a hole in the mist on the window and peered out. This was supposed to be a "New Town", but there was very little you could think of calling a *town*, and definitely nothing *new*, like a spaceport, or robots, or people flying past wearing jet-powered backpacks.

"Just think," said Mum, "a house, all to ourselves. You'll be able to have your own room, Philip."

Philip thought about it.

It would be nice not to have to share with Nan, he supposed. She snored like anything and once or twice, when he'd woken up in the night, he'd thought they'd been invaded by aliens.

"And we'll have an inside lav," said Dad, "no more pots under the bed!"

"All modern," agreed Mum, with a blissful sigh, "even a bath with a hot water tap. Oh, it'll be lovely."

It didn't *look* lovely. Philip had known the place wouldn't be as space-age as *Dan Dare*, really, but this wasn't even anything like as modern as the Festival of Britain exhibition that was being built in London. That was going to have a Dome of Discovery with all sorts of new inventions in it.

"This is our stop," said Dad.

And Philip jumped down from the bus and straight into a huge swamp of mud.

Dad tip-toed gingerly through the reddish mud, counting the squares of pegged string that marked out the building plots.

"Here we are," he said, "our new house."

Philip and Mum stood with the rain dripping down their necks and looked.

"It's just a muddy hole," said Philip.

Mum smiled bravely. "Well, it's not built yet," she said. "It'll be lovely when it's finished, I expect."

Dad scratched his head.

"Perhaps there'll be some information at the office, dear," he said. "We'll go and ask, and Phil can have a look round."

Philip did look around as they went away. He sighed. Now he came to think about it, this place was actually *very* like something from *Dan Dare* ... one of the nastier bits of the moon, perhaps.

"You're mad to want to move out of London," Nan had told Dad that morning. "It won't be all nice pavements, you know, it'll be all nasty mud. It'll be like a big bomb site."

"Just like home," Dad had replied grimly, as they'd set off.

Philip was trudging along the plaited puddles left by the tyres of the lorries when a voice shouted "Oi!" and something hit him on the side of his face.

Philip was just in time to see a figure dodging back inside one of the huge concrete drainage pipes that were lying about.

"Hey!" said Philip, indignantly. "What did you do that for?"

He wiped his face and found his hand smeared with mud.

"Go back to the smoke!" someone shouted.

Two figures appeared round an abandoned steamroller, and now there were squelchy footsteps behind Philip, too. He looked round for Mum and Dad, but they'd disappeared.

Philip found himself surrounded by two boys and a girl. They had muddy knees and hands and they looked unfriendly.

"You're a *Londoner*," sneered the girl.

"Yeah," said one of the boys, "all pale and weedy."

The other boy looked at him closely.

"Do you have black bogies?" he asked.

Philip blinked at him in surprise. Everyone had black bogies, didn't they? It was because of the sooty smoke from the coal fires that you breathed in all the time. He sniffed experimentally – but all he could smell here was damp earth.

"Hey, is that the new *Eagle*?" asked the first boy. "Let's see!" And while Philip was hesitating the girl had sneaked up behind him, snatched it from his pocket and they'd all run off.

Philip was about to give chase when Mum's voice called his name.

"We've been looking at the plans for the houses," she said, smiling through the drizzle. "Oh, they're going to be wonderful. Plastic worktops! And a whole square of shops."

Dad grinned at Philip.

"The clean air's done Phil good already," he said, looking at Philip's hot and angry face. "He's got a lovely healthy colour."

Philip found his *Eagle* dumped in the waste bin by the bus stop, which was something.

But he didn't feel comfortable until he came up from the Underground and saw the cranes over the Festival of Britain site. That was when he knew he was back in the middle of London. Back where he belonged.

Nan sniffed when Dad told her about the new house.

"Promises, promises," she muttered, as she squirted their shoes with disinfectant to kill all the country germs. "Ten to one they'll never build it. If you had any sense you'd stay in London with your friends and family, where it's civilised."

Philip went and sat by the fire. Nan was right about the New Town – it was just a nasty swamp, and the other children were going to hate him.

"It wasn't anything like as nice as London," he said. But neither Mum nor Dad took any notice.

2. THE TIME BOMB

"What was your new house like?" asked Philip's best friend Barry on Monday.

"Horrible," growled Philip. "It was nothing but a hole."

"Really? It was *underground*? Wow!"

Philip was about to reply, but Mr Archer was frowning at him from the front of the class so Philip hurriedly dipped his pen into the inkwell on his desk and copied the word INVENTIONS into his exercise book.

"Right," said Mr Archer, "now, who can name a new invention? Yes, Felicity?"

"Sir, my uncle's got a *television*," announced Felicity.

Barry started flailing his hand in the air.

"Yes, Barry?"

"Sir, televisions are rubbish! Going to the pictures is miles better. Television's really tiny and black and white, and everything always looks as if it's snowing."

"I see. Well, how about a really marvellous invention, then?" asked Mr Archer.

Philip put up his hand.

"Jet-powered backpacks, sir," he said.

Mr Archer blinked at Philip through his glasses, but now hands were waving all over the classroom.

"Spaceships, sir," said someone. "And cosmic ray guns."

"I think you've been reading too many comics," said Mr Archer. "How about something more practical?"

"But sir, please sir, ray guns *are* practical," said Barry, "especially if we get invaded by aliens."

Mr Archer blinked some more.

"Well," he said, slowly, "I suppose that's just what's happening at the moment, isn't it? We're being invaded by aliens. And they are the ones who are creating the time bomb."

The children's mouths fell open.

"Aliens, sir?" echoed Barry. "A *time bomb*?"

"I'm afraid so," said Mr Archer, gravely, "right here in London."

No one was sure whether to be more frightened or excited.

"Think of the huge numbers of large-headed, big-eyed creatures that have arrived in the city over the last few years," Mr Archer went on. "Why, Mrs Archer has had two herself!"

"Babies!" said Felicity, suddenly understanding.

"Yes, babies. So everyone's squashed together tighter and tighter until ... until what?"

"Until they explode, sir?" asked Barry, agog.

Everybody laughed.

"Well, we wouldn't want that," said Mr Archer, "so we need some inventions to solve the problem of there being lots more people, don't we?"

He turned back to the blackboard and wrote: THE TOWN OF THE FUTURE.

Philip made up some stuff about moving pavements and walkie-talkies, but he didn't believe a word of it.

Other people could move out, but he was never going to live in a stupid New Town. *Never*.

Barry and Philip usually went home from school through the bomb site. You could scramble through from one street to another without going along the road, as long as no one saw you.

The bomb site was great. There were bits of wall to hide behind while you fought space monsters and there was stuff like old chair legs to use as ray guns. Once Philip had even found a mixing bowl that had made a brilliant space helmet.

"Great Scott, Digby!" said Philip. He was being Dan Dare, while Barry was being Dan Dare's faithful servant. "I recognise this place. We've crash-landed in Mekonta. The place will soon be swarming with those nasty green-faced Treens."

"Oo-er!" said Barry. "Oh flip, Phil. Look!"

"It's not my arch-enemy the Mekon, is it, Digby?" said Philip, keeping up the game.

Barry gulped, and pointed a wavering finger.

"No," he said. "Phil, look! That ... that metal thing."

Philip looked. The rain had washed away a new layer of soil and ...

"Oh," he said.

Barry gulped again.

"It looks ... it looks like a bomb, doesn't it?" he said in a small voice.

Philip stood with one foot frozen in the air. People still quite often found unexploded bombs around and the slightest thing could set them off.

"What should we do?" quavered Barry.

Philip's heart went thump-thump-thump-thump.

"We'll have to tell the police," he said, putting his foot down very, very carefully.

Barry looked even more frightened than before.

"But Mr Archer said that anyone who was caught messing about on bomb sites would get the slipper!"

Philip hesitated. Then he reached out very slowly and got hold of a bit of wood.

"Get behind the wall," he whispered. "I'm going to dig round it so we can see what it is."

Barry put his fingers in his ears.

"Just be careful," he said. "Really, really, *really* careful."

Philip dug the bit of wood gently into the wet soil. Something orange appeared on the shining metal ... and then the letters F and R.

"Fritz," whispered Barry. "That's a German name. It *is* a bomb!"

There was a C visible, now. And an O, and then ...

"Cocoa!" Philip yelled in triumph, jumping up. "It's an old tin of Fry's cocoa!"

A head poked out of a nearby window and Philip and Barry ran away, laughing, and didn't stop running until they got home.

London was brilliant, thought Philip, as he climbed the stairs to the flat. Really exciting.

Nan was singing "Maybe it's because I'm a Londoner" as she made a swede pie for supper. Philip joined in loudly. He was just going to *have* to get Mum and Dad to change their minds about moving.

Philip got his chance to start his staying-in-London campaign when he went Saturday morning shopping with Mum.

"What nice shops," he kept saying. "Streets and streets full of them. What a lot of choice."

Mum gave him a look.

"All right," she said, "if you're enjoying it that much, we'll go up Oxford Street."

Mum spent *hours* looking at skinny-waisted dresses. It nearly killed him. To make matters worse, he knew she wasn't going to buy anything because she was saving up for things for the new house.

"If we weren't moving you could buy loads of clothes," he said, "especially now they're not rationed any more."

It started raining as they were going home, but a big red double-decker bus came along almost straight away.

"It's a good job we didn't have to wait ages, like we did in the country," said Philip, pointedly.

"Yes," said Mum. "You know, when we move out of London, I think we'll have to get bicycles."

Philip stared at her, open-mouthed, as she paid the conductor.

"*Bicyles?*" he said.

Mum smiled. "Won't that be nice?"

A bicycle! Philip had never even *dreamt* of owning his own bicycle. But he took a deep breath and banished visions of free-wheeling joyfully downhill.

"Not as nice as staying in London," he said firmly.

3. RAGS AND BONES

It was lucky that Philip wasn't the only one who thought that moving out was a terrible idea.

"I've got us some nice eels," said Nan, breaking off for a moment from singing "Maybe it's because I'm a Londoner" again as she served up supper. "Fresh from the river. You'd miss those if you moved out."

"There'll be all sorts of fresh stuff in the country," said Mum, swiftly.

Nan sniffed.

"You're telling me! Poisonous mushrooms and berries. Not to mention the wolves and all sorts. You won't be able to get your milk off the doorstep without worrying you'll be savaged."

Mum glared at her.

"You know, I heard scurrying earlier," she said to Dad. "I'm afraid there's a rat in the roof. You're never far from rats in London."

Nan snorted.

"Rats? That'll just be the pigeons stamping about. You wait until you get to the country. You'll have more than rats to worry about then."

Philip looked at Dad. If he had a bicycle then he'd probably be quite safe from wolves. But still ...

Dad winked at him.

"We'll go down to the library and look it all up tomorrow," he said. "Anyway, nothing could be worse than some of the dogs round here."

"Or some of the people," said Mum, tartly.

According to the copy of *Animals of Britain* in the library, there were no wolves in England. But there were stags with huge antlers and pike that could have your arm off, as well as poisonous snakes.

"It sounds dangerous," said Philip, as they walked home. In the distance he could hear the mournful howling of the rag-and-bone man as he drove his horse and cart along. *Rag-gyBOH,* he went. *Rag-gyBOH.*

"It's not really," said Dad. "After all, lots of people live in the country, and they don't come to any harm. It'll be safer in lots of ways. Cleaner air, for one thing, and –"

But Dad never finished what he was saying because he was interrupted by a piercing whinny and a great crashing of hooves, and then the rapid *clop-clop, clop-clop* of a galloping horse.

Cars were pulling over to the side of the road as the horse came charging round the corner with the rag-and-bone man's cart bumping and slewing about behind it.

"Watch out!" shouted Dad.

He pushed Philip into the safety of a doorway and ran forwards across the street.

Behind the cart a Stop-Me-And-Buy-One ice-cream man was pedalling along as fast as he could in pursuit, while behind him the little rag-and-bone man was running along shouting, *"Whoa! Hercules! Whoa!"*

The horse was almost level with Philip now, and Dad was throwing himself forwards and catching hold of the horse's bridle.

But the horse was strong and very scared, and Dad was carried along hanging on for dear life, because if he fell he might be trampled by the iron-shod hooves, or crushed by a cartwheel.

Philip began to run along the pavement. Whatever happened, he had to be there.

Dad's weight was slowing the horse down a bit and Philip began to think everything would soon be over, but then he realised that the horse was heading for the main road – the main road and the *tramline*.

Dad must have seen the danger almost at the same moment Philip did, because he looked across, saw the great caterpillar of the tram coming along and shouted: *"The brake! Someone put on the brake!"*

The Stop-Me-And-Buy-One man had been flagging, but now he put on a tremendous spurt and managed to get a hand on the cart's brake.

Sparks flew from the wheels as the brakes slammed on and the horse, suddenly noticing the tram in front of him, reared up and whinnied again. By the time Philip had shaken the sound out of his head, several passers-by had grabbed hold of the horse's harness and the horse was standing still, panting and shivering all over.

"It was a bloomin' pigeon frightened him," explained the little rag-and-bone man, angrily, as he stroked the horse's foam-flecked neck. "Came down out of nowhere and landed on his nose!"

"Don't tell Mum," Dad said to Philip, on the way home; but Mum had already heard all about it from Mrs Grainger down the street.

"You might have been killed," Mum said, though her eyes were sparkling proudly. "You might have been dragged under the wheels."

"Flipping pigeons," grumbled Nan. "One *went* on my head the other day when I was putting the clothes through the mangle."

"Think what would have happened if that poor horse had crashed into the tram," said Mum.

"Terrible dangerous things, trams," said Nan.

Dad grinned at Philip. "Well," he said, "at least we'll be safe from trams once we're in the country. Won't we, Phil?"

"Bah!" said Nan.

But Philip couldn't help admitting to himself that Dad was probably right.

4. OLD LAMPS FOR NEW

The rain went on and on; sometimes even the pigeons began to sound as if they were gargling. Nan kept knitting jumpers and socks for the family.

"You'll need warm clothes out in the country," she said.

Dad rolled his eyes. "But we're only moving 20 miles, Mother."

"It's still colder than London. All the smoke here keeps us warm. You just don't know when you're well off, you don't."

"But New Towns are the future, Mother."

"Yes," said Mum, loyally. "Remember what the King said when they started building on the Festival of Britain site? 'The future holds many opportunities for us.'"

"But the King isn't moving out, is he?" snapped Nan. "He could live anywhere, God bless him, but he's happy in London. They should be building houses here, not wasting money on a silly festival."

Dad coughed and choked. The chimney always smoked when the wind was in the north.

"Well, *I'd* stay if I could live in Buckingham Palace," he muttered darkly, as he went out to work.

"That's right," said Mum, on her way down to the yard to put some wet washing through the mangle.

Philip finished his porridge. Down the road a lorry was coughing and coughing, too, as the driver tried to start it.

"Listen to that," said Nan, giving Philip his satchel. "They should have stuck with good old starting handles to make the engines go, not all these new-fangled push-button things that just make them sound as if they've got bronchitis. The whole country's going to the dogs. It's all these television rays, frying everyone's brains."

As she said it, every light in all the streets and houses winked off. Another power cut.

"And there was nothing wrong with gas lamps, either!" Nan finished up in triumph, as Philip opened the door to go to school.

When Philip arrived, Felicity was still going on and on about her uncle's television.

"Good old Muffin, Muffin the Mule!" she sang, as they waited in the playground for Mr Archer to ring the bell for the start of morning lessons.

"That sounds rubbish," said Barry, turning up his collar against the rain.

Felicity stuck out her tongue. "You're just jealous 'cause you haven't got a television!"

"*Jealous*? Why should I want to watch a stupid black and white donkey puppet that doesn't do anything?"

"It *does* do things! And anyway, it's a mule, not a donkey. It dances about on the piano while the lady sings. So there!"

Barry and Philip looked at each other in disbelief.

"Television is newfangled rubbish," said Philip, stoutly, "and the invisible television rays fry your brains. Radio is miles better. You get brilliant things on the radio like *The War of the Worlds*. Radios are tried and tested."

And then he suddenly started listening to himself and realised to his horror that he'd turned into his nan.

Philip and Barry didn't feel like playing on the bomb site, so they played football on the way home instead.

"Dad says *we're* going to move out in the summer," said Barry. "We're going to a New Town just like you. Mum says there'll be loads of places to play, but I don't know if I'll like it."

Philip hesitated.

"I'd really miss London if we moved," he said.

Barry frowned. "It might be all right if we moved to the same place," he suggested.

"Yes," agreed Philip, "and it'd be all right if everyone had jet-powered backpacks like in *Dan Dare*."

"Yeah," said Barry, "I'd go faster than a rocket!"

He took a wild kick at the tennis ball they were playing with and it bounced high up over Philip's outstretched foot, neatly over some railings, then down into someone's basement area. They went to peer down at it, but a lady shook her fist at them, so they walked sadly away.

"There's nowhere to play round here," said Barry, bitterly. "The country would be better for that."

"No, it wouldn't," said Philip and told Barry about the children who'd stolen his comic.

"But you did get it back," pointed out Barry.

"Only from a waste bin!"

"Yes, the waste bin at your bus stop where you were bound to find it. And it wasn't torn up, was it?"

"I suppose not," admitted Philip, "but the place was still just a load of mud."

They found a tin can and played football with that until a car came along and squashed it flat.

"Flipping cars!" said Philip. "There's one comes along practically every minute nowadays."

"That was a Jaguar Mark VII," said Barry, gazing after it, wistfully. "The new model. Cor! Wouldn't it be great to ride in one of them."

"It'd be all right," said Philip grudgingly, as they split up to go home.

The flat was hung round with so much washing that there was hardly anywhere to sit. Mum flung up her hands at the sight of him.

"I just don't know how you manage to get your knees so grubby!" she exclaimed. "Oh, *and* the copper's broken again so there's no hot water!"

When Dad got home Philip was squatting in a kettleful of hot water in the tub in front of the fire.

"Oh, what an awful day!" wailed Mum.

Dad hugged her. "Never mind," he said, "when we've got our own house we'll buy a washing machine."

"But that's months in the future!" said Mum.

"If it ever happens," said Nan, sourly. "Anyway, damp air's good for the lungs, everyone knows that. Even better than smoking."

Dad winked at Philip.

"Well, whatever happens, we definitely need a treat," he said. "A proper tonic. I'll tell you what, I'll get us tickets for the Festival of Britain exhibition. It opens at the beginning of May. Then we'll *really* be able to see what the future holds."

5. THE FUTURE

"Here we are," said Dad, "the Festival of Britain!"

"Ooh, isn't it marvellous," said Mum. "Look at all the colours. Ooh, and look at that, a display of lamp posts! And before you even get through the gates, too."

"Look at that folding one, Phil," said Dad, "that's so they can change the light bulbs easily."

"Whatever next?" said Mum.

The place was crowded with happy and excited people hurrying through the entrance.

And there, right in front of them, was an enormous metal dome – like a space station.

Philip's jaw dropped with amazement.

"The Dome of Discovery, that is," said Dad.

"Can we go in?"

"Of course we can," said Dad.

They pushed their way through the smartly dressed crowds. There were young people, old people – and even one group of people who must have been from another country. They seemed to be enjoying themselves hugely.

"They're from the West Indies, I expect," said Dad. "Quite a lot of people from there are coming to live in England."

Philip thought the whole exhibition was terrific, even before they turned a corner and saw a pen-shaped tower that seemed to float in the air.

"A spaceship!" exclaimed Philip.

"The Skylon Tower," read Dad from the guidebook.

Philip walked right underneath it, feeling like Dan Dare as he looked up along its shining sides.

"Will our New Town be like this?" he asked.

Mum and Dad looked at each other and laughed.

"Perhaps not quite as modern as this," said Dad.

"Ooh, I wouldn't want to live in that tower," said Mum. "Think of having to sweep all those stairs!"

Philip sighed.

"But will we have jet-powered backpacks?" he asked.

"Well, perhaps we will, one day," said Dad. "By the year 2000, who can tell what our lives will be like?"

"There might be a machine that *dries* clothes," said Mum, wistfully, "and meals you buy ready-made, that just need to be heated up."

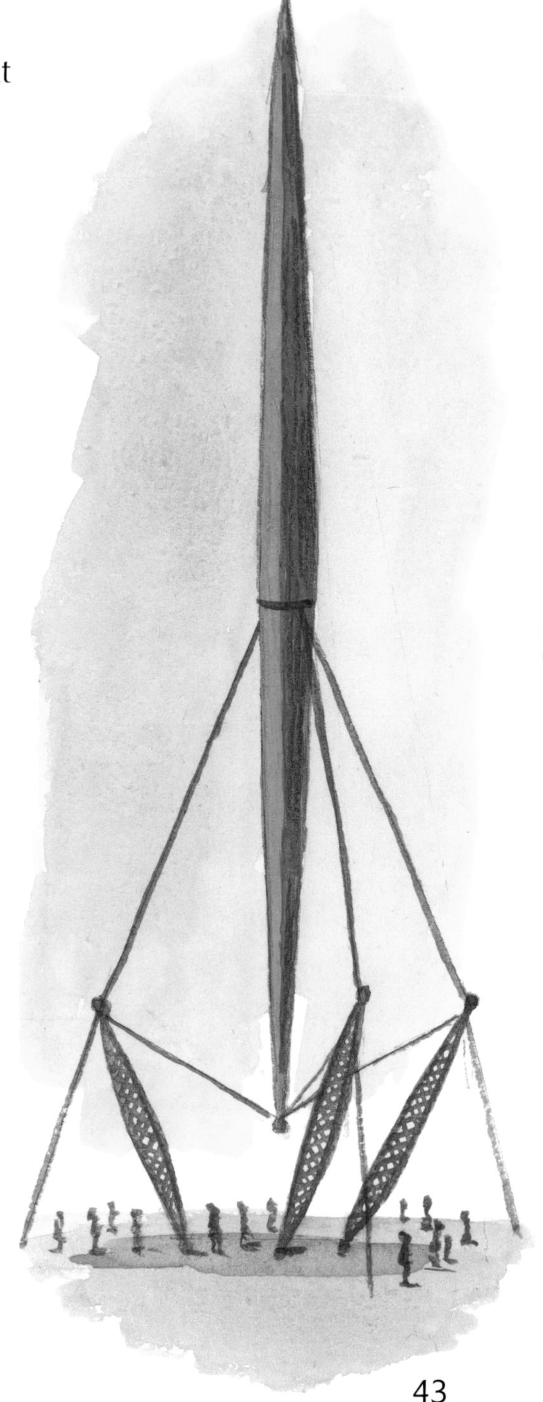

"And television in colour with space adventures on it," said Philip.

"And a telephone you can carry about in your pocket," said Dad, "and an electric book that can tell you anything."

But Philip shook his head. "That would have to be magic," he said.

There was so much to see that Philip got dizzy. There was a radar display of the boats on the river and strange windows that showed you the stars and planets.

At lunchtime, Philip's glass of milk was cold. Really, really cold, even though it was quite warm outside.

"From a refrigerator," explained Dad. "Right. The Lion and Unicorn Pavilion next."

The Lion and Unicorn Pavilion didn't have any lions or unicorns in it, but there was a violin made entirely out of old matchsticks. Philip looked round to ask Mum and Dad why anyone would want to make such a thing ... and found they weren't there.

Philip went all round the pavilion, searching for Mum and Dad, but there were thousands of people everywhere. Should he stay where he was, or go outside?

He didn't have any money to get the bus home, or to telephone Mrs Grainger along the street.

"Are you all right, young man?" asked a voice, as Philip hesitated. "You look a bit lost."

It was one of the men from the West Indies.

"Well," said Philip, "I'm not *lost*, exactly. I mean, I know where I am."

That made the man laugh.

"But you've lost your mother and father, right?"

Philip nodded.

"Well," said the man, "I'll tell you what we'll do. We'll wait by the entrance to the pavilion and if your mother and father don't come soon, then we'll ask a policeman. OK?"

Philip, very relieved, followed the man to the entrance. "There are just so many people here," he explained.

"You're telling me. When I first came to England the crowds nearly made my head spin right off my shoulders."

"Have you come from somewhere a long way away?" asked Philip.

"That's right. My name is Mr Johnson and I come from Jamaica."

Philip thought about all the hundreds of miles Mr Johnson had come.

"Weren't you worried about coming to live in a strange place?" he asked.

Mr Johnson laughed again.

"If I'd been any more worried, I reckon all my hair would have fallen out."

"So why did you come?"

"Partly to find work," he answered, "but mostly for the adventure, I suppose."

"And ... has it been a good adventure, Mr Johnson?"

Mr Johnson smiled at him.

"Well, there's been good bits and bad bits. Good and bad people, too. But I wouldn't have been happy if I hadn't seized the adventure."

"PHILIP!"

Mum came rushing up to them.

"I thought we'd lost you for good," she said, clasping him to her. "We thought you were following us, but it turned out to be another boy in a jumper just like yours. Oh, you must have been so worried!"

"It was all right," said Philip. "Mr Johnson's been looking after me. He's been telling me about moving to England."

Dad shook hands with Mr Johnson and thanked him very much indeed.

"My pleasure," said Mr Johnson. "Enjoy the rest of your day!"

They did. They saw the Guinness clock strike the hour and bought a pen which seemed, oddly, to work with *solid* ink.

"It's a ballpoint pen. Not nearly so messy as an ordinary pen," said Mum, admiring it.

But at last it was time to go home. Mum looked at all the lively people around her, pushing and laughing and happy.

"I really do love living in London," she said, sadly, "but we've got to move out, haven't we? We can't let a chance like this go."

"That's right," said Dad. "We've got to seize the opportunity."

Philip thought about the children who'd taken his comic. And all the mud.

But then he thought about Mr Johnson. "Seize the adventure," he'd said.

Halfway home, Mum suddenly said, "Oh, but poor Nan. I know she thinks New Towns will be dreadful places, but do you really think she'll be happy on her own?"

"Everything's changing so fast," said Dad. "It's difficult for the old people."

Philip was half asleep.

"Nan's not that old," he murmured. "She ought to seize the adventure, too."

"So it's definite, then," growled Nan when they got home, glowering at them. "You're leaving London. *And* all your friends and everything."

"Well, we hope not," said Dad. "Look, we know you love London and lived here all through the Blitz, but we want you to move out, too. So we'll still be close."

"You've just got to come, Nan," said Philip. "We won't ever be able to manage without you, will we?"

Nan stared at them all.

"They're building bungalows out there," said Dad, "especially for people on their own."

"A bungalow? Near you?" echoed Nan.

"With an inside toilet and bath and everything," said Mum.

Nan sniffed.

"Well, I suppose it'll be something not to have to share with Philip," she conceded. "Him and his snoring!"

And then Nan thought some more, and she said, "You know, if I'm moving out, I think I'll have to get myself a bicycle."

They moved in the summer, in time for Philip to start at his new school. One really good thing was that it turned out that Barry's family was moving to the same town, so he would be there, too.

Felicity's family was moving to a town in Kent.

"It's a *much* better town than *your* one," she said, smugly. And Philip felt jolly glad to be moving in the opposite direction.

Philip climbed down the stairs from the flat for the last time.

"I'll always be a Londoner," said Nan. "Best place in the world, London. Ooh, but it will be nice not to have to carry coal up and down those flipping stairs."

They turned away and walked to the bus stop.

Philip had a new *Eagle* comic to read on the way. *Dan Dare,* it said, *Pilot of the Future*. Philip sighed happily and began to read.

Reasons for moving to a New Town

1 not sharing a room with Nan

2 having lots of room to play in the country

3 getting a new house with:
   a) washing machine so Mum doesn't get hot and bothered on washing day
   b) a ground floor so we don't have to carry up coal from downstairs
   c) bathroom indoors with bath and hot water
   d) lavatory indoors

4 getting a bicycle

5 being close to Barry

6 getting away from Felicity

7 too much traffic in London

Reasons for NOT leaving London

1 not having exciting places to go, like the Festival of Britain

2 children being unfriendly in a New Town because I'm a stranger

3 Nan not wanting to move

4 not wanting to leave all the people I know

5 not having bomb sites to play on

6 not so many buses and big shops

7 countryside could be dangerous

Ideas for guided reading

Learning objectives: understand underlying themes, causes and points of view; sustain engagement with longer texts using different techniques; use a range of oral techniques to present persuasive arguments

Curriculum links: History: How life in Britain has changed since 1948; Citizenship: Moving on, Choices

Interest words: blitz, dilemma, indignantly, experimentally, pointedly, loyally, newfangled, grudgingly

Resources: images of post-war Britain, information about New Towns, ICT

Getting started

This book can be read over two or more guided reading sessions.

- Read the blurb together. Ask children to discuss what the story will be about and what the key themes may be.
- Describe the Blitz and the post-war London context if children are not familiar with this.
- Ask children to read chapter 1 silently.
- Discuss the key events in chapter 1. List what is known about Philip's character and what can be inferred.

Reading and responding

- Ask children to read chapter 1 again to identify the main characters' (Mum, Dad, Nan, Philip) points of view about leaving London to live in a New Town.
- Ask each child to go into role as a character and describe their point of view and reasons for wanting/not wanting to move.
- In pairs, children go into role as Philip and his friend, with Philip recounting his visit to the New Town to Barry.
- Ask children to continue reading the story, noticing how Philip's point of view about moving to the New Town alters as the story develops.